This igloo book belongs to:

...............................................................

"Hello, my name is Rosy.
Come and see what happens
to my shiny, star balloon."

Published in 2011
by Igloo Books Ltd
Cottage Farm
Sywell
NN6 0BJ
www.igloo-books.com

L006 0811

2 4 6 8 10 9 7 5 3 1

ISBN: 978-0-85734-817-3

Printed and manufactured in China

# Rosy's
## Lost
# Balloon

Alex Michaels

Illustrated by
Steve Whitlow

igloo

One day, in summer, Rosy
got a shiny, star balloon.

"It's very special," said her mother.
"It's a present from the moon."

Rosy's lovely, bright, balloon
floated in the air.

She held it by a ribbon
and took it everywhere.

All too soon, the sunshine went
and the wind began to blow.

It tugged at Rosy's star balloon.
"Hold on tight, Rosy. Don't let go!"

The rough wind blew and storm clouds grew
and Rosy could not hold on.

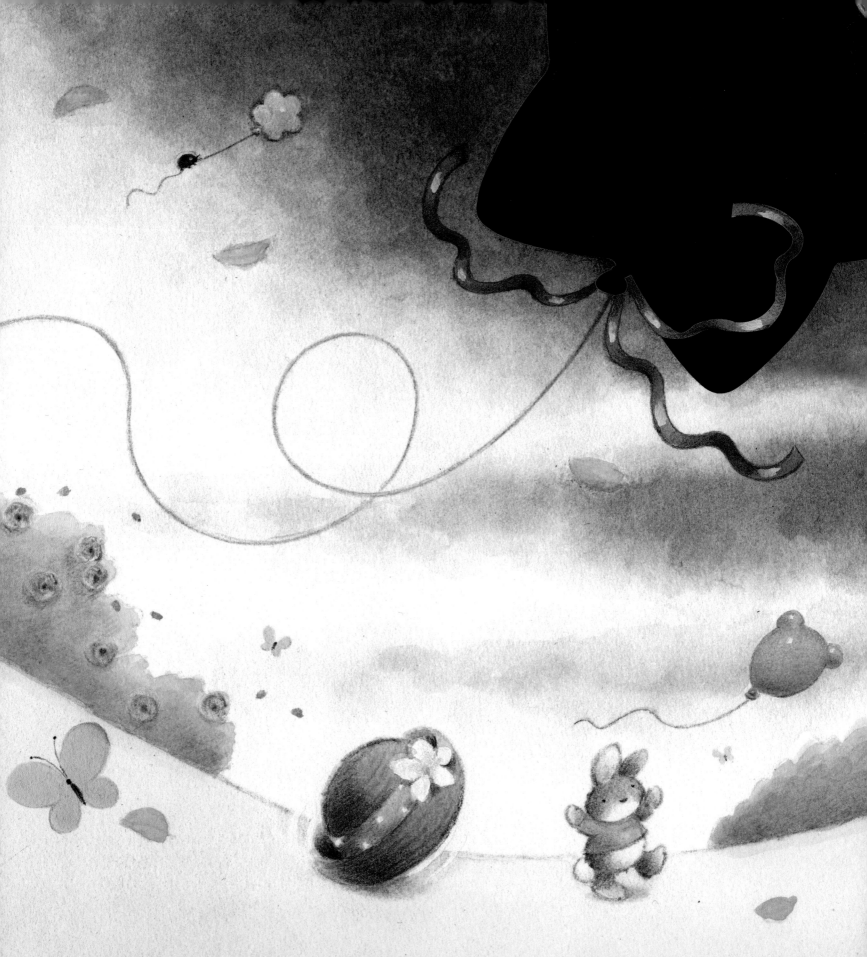

Whoosh! went the wind, it tugged and pulled.
Suddenly, the star balloon was gone.

"Give it back!" cried Rosy, as the red ribbon trailed,
but the cruel wind seemed to laugh.

It whistled and whooshed and roughly
pushed the balloon along the path.

Up, up, went the balloon,
to the tallest tree top.

It's red ribbon tangled and
the star balloon stopped.

"Caw," went the crow, with his feathers so sleek.
Suddenly, he took the ribbon in his beak.

Off he flew, into the stormy sky
and carried the star balloon up high.

Suddenly, lightning crashed
and thunder clapped.
The crow's feathers ruffled
and his blue wings flapped.

"Caw, Caw!" cried the crow
and let the star balloon go.

Up, up, went the balloon,
past the clouds, past the rain.

"My star balloon is gone," sobbed Rosy,
"I'll never see it again."

"There, there," said her mother, holding Rosy tight,
as the soft, sunlight gave way to the night.

Rosy's mother said that the moon was alone
and he cried for the star balloon to come home.

"Look up," she said. "Look up high.
There's your star balloon, twinkling in the sky."

"Goodnight," said Rosy. "I'll see you soon,"
and she blew a kiss to her special, star balloon.
"Goodnight, Rosy. Sleep tight."

"Goodbye,
See you soon!"

# Watch out for more fantastic stories in the igloo picture book range!

## Detective Ted

An ordinary teddy turns detective to solve the mystery of who is eating all the cookies at night.

## Fly, Freddy, Fly

There are thrills and spills galore in this touching story about a penguin who is desperate to fly.

## Ellie's Magic Wish

Follow Ellie as she twirls in a world of imagination and sparkles. It's pure fairy heaven!

**igloo**